T0012450

GRIZZLY BEAR VS. WOLF PACK

BY NATHAN SOMMER

BELLWETHER MEDIA • MINNEAPOLIS, MN

TM

Torque brims with excitement
perfect for thrill-seekers of all kinds.
Discover daring survival skills, explore
uncharted worlds, and marvel at mighty
engines and extreme sports. In *Torque* books,
anything can happen. Are you ready?

This edition first published in 2020 by Bellwether Media, Inc.

Library of Congress Cataloging-in-Publication Data

Names: Sommer, Nathan, author.
Title: Grizzly Bear vs. Wolf Pack / by Nathan Sommer.
  Other titles: Grizzly bear versus wolf pack
Description: Minneapolis, MN : Bellwether Media, Inc., 2020. | Series:
  Torque: animal battles | Includes bibliographical references and index.
  | Audience: Ages 7-12 | Audience: Grades 3-7 | Summary: "Amazing
  photography accompanies engaging information about the fighting
  abilities of grizzly bears and wolves. The combination of high-interest
  subject matter and light text is intended for students in grades 3
  through 7"– Provided by publisher.
Identifiers: LCCN 2019030402 (print) | LCCN 2019030403 (ebook) |
  ISBN 9781644871584 (library binding) | ISBN 9781618918383 (ebook)
Subjects: LCSH: Grizzly bear–Juvenile literature. | Wolves–Juvenile literature.
Classification: LCC QL737.C27 S6393 2020 (print) | LCC QL737.C27 (ebook)
  | DDC 599.784–dc23
LC record available at https://lccn.loc.gov/2019030402
LC ebook record available at https://lccn.loc.gov/2019030403

Editor: Christina Leaf   Designer: Andrea Schneider

Printed in the United States of America, North Mankato, MN.

TABLE OF CONTENTS

THE COMPETITORS

Grizzly bears top many food chains. These fearsome beasts can hunt whatever they want. Standing up to 8 feet (2.4 meters) tall, the bears have few enemies.

Wolves challenge grizzly bears as top **predators** in many **habitats**. These great runners and swimmers give most **prey** no chance for escape. It is a knockout fight when grizzlies and wolves come together!

Grizzly bears bulk up to store energy before sleeping all winter. They eat so much in the fall that some gain 3 pounds (1.4 kilograms) a day!

Grizzly bears are **mammals** with strong bodies. They have humped shoulders and sharp claws. Their name comes from their long, silvery **guard hairs**. These give the bears a **grizzled** look.

Grizzlies are a **subspecies** of brown bear. They roam mountainous forests and frozen **tundra**. Adults live alone but sometimes feed in groups. The beasts **hibernate** in winter months.

GRIZZLY BEAR PROFILE

HEIGHT
UP TO 8 FEET
(2.4 METERS)

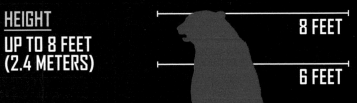

8 FEET

6 FEET

WEIGHT
UP TO
900 POUNDS
(408 KILOGRAMS)

4 FEET

2 FEET

HABITAT

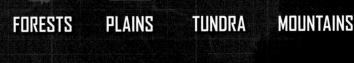

FORESTS   PLAINS   TUNDRA   MOUNTAINS

GRIZZLY BEAR RANGE

RANGE

WOLF PROFILE

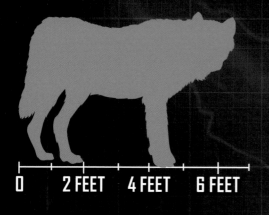

LENGTH
UP TO 6.5 FEET
(2 METERS)

WEIGHT
UP TO
130 POUNDS
(59 KILOGRAMS)

0   2 FEET   4 FEET   6 FEET

HABITAT

WOODLANDS   TUNDRA   PLAINS   DESERTS

WOLF RANGE

■ RANGE

Wolves are the largest type of wild dog. They have long, bushy tails and are black, gray, or white. These social mammals live in packs of around 20.

Wolves travel and hunt as a team. Working together, they can bring down large prey like moose and elk! The predators **adapt** to live wherever there is plenty of food.

MEAT LOVERS

Wolves value every meal they can get. They eat as much as 20 pounds (9 kilograms) in one sitting!

SECRET WEAPONS

Grizzlies use senses to their **advantage**. They can smell **carrion** from 18 miles (29 kilometers) away! Their rounded ears focus on faraway sounds to hear incoming danger.

WOLF

SHARP TEETH

POWERFUL JAWS

ENERGY

Wolves have strength in numbers. They talk to each other using different noises. Barks and howls call the pack together to take on enemies.

SECRET WEAPONS

STRONG
HEARING

STRONG SENSE
OF SMELL

STRENGTH

CLAWS

Grizzlies have super strength. They can lift more than 700 pounds (317 kilograms)! They are also fast. These beasts reach speeds of 35 miles (56 kilometers) per hour.

Wolves have energy that tires even the strongest animals. Packs search for prey over hundreds of miles. They can hit speeds of up to 38 miles (61 kilometers) per hour!

GRIZZLY CLAWS

Thick grizzly claws grow up to 4 inches (10 centimeters) long. Grizzlies use these to dig and fight. They can swipe fish right out of water!

	GRIZZLY CLAWS	WOLF TEETH	PENNY
4 INCHES	4"		
3 INCHES			
2 INCHES		2.5"	
1 INCH			
0			.75"

Wolves have powerful teeth and jaws that cut through skin in just one bite. These can even break bones! Their sharp **canine teeth** grow up to 2.5 inches (6.3 centimeters) long.

ATTACK MOVES

Grizzlies growl and pound their paws on the ground when angry. They charge at enemies if challenged. This is enough to scare most away. If not, grizzlies are ready to battle!

Wolves fight to protect their packs. Groups of them often circle enemies. This gives most threats no chance to escape. Then, the pack attacks together.

HABITAT DEFENDERS

Wolves are very defensive of their habitats. They will attack any animal they see as a danger to their home.

Grizzlies fight every animal that tries to attack them. Their super strength and sharp claws help them out. One or two powerful swats is enough to kill most enemies.

BEAR VS. BEAR

Grizzlies are not against fighting other bears. They will kill other grizzlies if it comes down to a meal.

Wolves hunt to live. They mostly use sharp teeth as weapons to tear enemies apart slowly. One bite to the neck can **paralyze** attackers.

READY, FIGHT!

A wolf and a grizzly circle carrion. They must get through one another to earn their meal. The grizzly swats and injures the wolf. Wolves are no match for grizzlies one-on-one.

But the hurt wolf yelps to alert its pack. The grizzly is soon swarmed! They tear the bear apart bit by bit as a team. Wolves remain top dog today!

GLOSSARY

adapt—to get used to different conditions easily

advantage—something an animal has or can do better than their enemy

canine teeth—long, pointed teeth that are often the sharpest in the mouth

carrion—the remains of a dead animal

grizzled—streaked with gray

guard hairs—long, thick hairs that trap heat to keep an animal warm

habitats—the homes or areas where animals prefer to live

hibernate—to spend the winter sleeping or resting

mammals—warm-blooded animals that have backbones and feed their young milk

paralyze—to make unable to move

predators—animals that hunt other animals for food

prey—animals that are hunted by other animals for food

subspecies—particular types of animals that exist within a species

tundra—a flat, treeless area where the ground is always frozen

TO LEARN MORE

AT THE LIBRARY

Daly, Ruth. *Bringing Back the Grizzly Bear*. New York, N.Y.: Crabtree Publishing, 2019.

Herrington, Lisa M. *Gray Wolves*. New York, N.Y.: Children's Press, 2019.

Krieger, Emily. *Animal Smackdown: Surprising Animal Matchups with Surprising Results*. Washington D.C.: National Geographic Kids, 2018.

ON THE WEB

FACTSURFER

Factsurfer.com gives you a safe, fun way to find more information.

1. Go to www.factsurfer.com

2. Enter "grizzly bear vs. wolf pack" into the search box and click Q.

3. Select your book cover to see a list of related web sites.

INDEX

The images in this book are reproduced through the courtesy of: Scott E Read, front cover (bear), pp. 6-7, 10, 12 (weapon 3), 20-21 (bear); costasd68/ Despositphotos, front cover (wolf); Dennis W Donohue, pp. 4, 14 (bear); Michael Roeder, p. 5; David Dirga, pp. 8-9; Andyworks, pp. 11 (wolves), 15; kochanowski, p. 11 (weapon 1); Bildagentur Zoonar GmbH, p. 11 (weapon 2); Micahl Ninger, p. 11 (weapon 3); Sergey Uryadnikov, p. 12 (bear); Nagel Photography, p. 12 (weapon 1, 2, 4); Michelle Lalancette, p. 13; TheWonderWays, p. 14 (claws); Jack Bell Photography, p. 16; Lori Ellis, p. 17; AndreAnita, p. 18; karlumbriaco, pp. 19, 20-21 (wolves, back); Marc Hermann, pp. 20-21 (wolves, front).